Santa Almost Missed Our Town

Written by Tom Christopher & David J. Fitzpatrick
Illustrated by Heather Reilly

Published by Reilly Books
At Createspace
www.reillybooks.com

ISBN: **978-0-9939758-0-6**

This book is dedicated to Tom's grandson Aaron,
and his nephew Rylan. Children keep the magic of Christmas
alive.

To Dave's grandchildren; Braxon, Kacie, Colin, and another grandchild
expected for April 2015. You mean the world to me.
To all children who help keep the magic of Christmas alive.

And for Marg & Dan Tietje, the holidays just wouldn't be the same

without family here to share it with.

This book features a musical cadence in its story, which comes from a
treasured song by local songwriters Tom Christopher & David J.
Fitzpatrick. Paired with brilliantly colourful images of the holiday
season, and memories past, we all hope you enjoy it.

It was just a year ago,
We had an awful fright,
It seemed that Santa might not
Find our town on Christmas night.

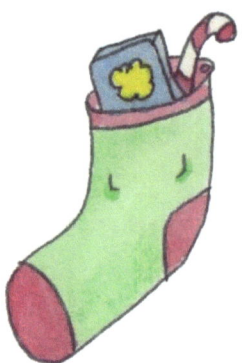

The forecast called for a storm
And the northerly winds to blow,
The snow was piling higher
As it dropped to 40 below.

It was the year that Santa
Almost missed our town
There was at least four feet
Of snow upon the ground.

The power lines went down,
Not one light to be found,
On the year that Santa
Almost missed our town.

The houses they were decorated,
But no Christmas glow,
Everybody's yard displays
Were covered up with snow.

The kids were all downhearted
Realizing their worst fear,
There was a chance that Santa
Wouldn't find our town this year.

It was the year that Santa
Almost missed our town
There was at least four feet
Of snow upon the ground.

The power lines went down,
Not one light to be found,
On the year that Santa
Almost missed our town.

Grandpa jumped up and cried
"I can't take this anymore!"
With that he made his way
Out through the basement door.

We all looked out at him
With amazement and surprise,
You could see the smile upon his face,
And a twinkle in his eyes.

That night was Christmas Eve,
We were heading off to bed,
We shuffled up the stairs,
And as we turned our head...

Looking out the window
His message was all so clear,
The solar lights out in the snow spelled:
SANTA, PLEASE STOP HERE!

It was the year that Santa
Almost missed our town
There was at least four feet
Of snow upon the ground.

The power lines went down,
Not one light to be found,
On the year that Santa
Almost missed our town.

SANTA
PLEASE
STOPHERE

**Other Albums by Tom Christopher
and David J. Fitzpatrick:**

D aNd A Vault One,

D aNd A "Yes Me Buddy"

The song *Santa Almost Missed Our Town*, which this book is based on, can be found on their album

D aNd A Christmas Vault Two

Learn more about the authors and their music at:
www.danda2010.com

Other books written and illustrated by Heather Reilly:

Novels:

Binding of the Almatraek Book I: *Knight's Surrender*
Binding of the Almatraek Book II: *Noble Pursuit*

Children's:

The Tree and the Sun
Tock-Tick-Tock, the Mouse and the Clock
The Poetical Alphabetical Book

Upcoming books:

Binding of the Almatraek Book III: *Enchanted Page*
The Words We See: Kindergarten Sight Words on the Rock

Learn more about the illustrator and her books at:
www.reillybooks.com

Titles are also available at amazon.com,
and novels on ebook at smashwords.com

Bios

Tom grew up in Mercer's Cove in the town of Bay Roberts, Newfoundland. His parents and family moved to Butlerville when he was in high school. After finishing high school he worked at various jobs such as fish plant worker, working in vegetable gardens, the Coca-Cola Distributors, also working on blueberry farms. Tom realized there was not enough work for a steady income so he moved to Toronto, Ontario.

Dave was born in Toronto, Ontario, and moved to Bay Roberts, Newfoundland and Labrador when he was five years old. He started playing guitar at age 7 and drums even before that. By the time he was ten years old, he had written and recorded his first song playing the drums, bass, guitars and doing lead and backing vocals. When he turned twelve years old, he started playing bars with his mother's favorite band "Black Magic".

Heather is the author of two medieval fantasy novels in a series that will consist of five, called the *Binding of the Almatraek*. She has also written and illustrated three other books for young children. With a background as a music teacher, she often emphasizes the use of rhyme or cadence in her books, and includes activities that parents, caregivers, and teachers can use with their child(ren). She currently lives in Dildo, Newfoundland, with her husband, and two small children.

www.ingramcontent.com/pod-product-compliance
Lightning Source LLC
Chambersburg PA
CBHW041543240626
47164CB00002B/116